Clouds of war are rolling in. . . .

"Could I do my project on dragons?" Song Lee begged.

Before Miss Mackle could say yes, Harry jumped up. "My grandmother read St. George and the Dragon *to me last night. It was cool. See?"* Harry whipped the library book out of his backpack. "I want to do dragons, too!"

Everyone looked at the terrifying beast on the cover. It was spitting fire.

"Hmmm . . ." the teacher replied. "Why not? They're mythical animals. You can both do dragons. You and Song Lee work so well together."

While Harry slapped Song Lee five, we all smiled. No one dreamed Miss Mackle's decision was going to be deadly.

I think the weather knew, though. Dark clouds circled Southeast School and thunder rolled. When a tree branch tapped our classroom window, we stopped talking and looked up. Was the whistling wind trying to tell us something?

BOOKS ABOUT
HORRIBLE HARRY AND SONG LEE

Horrible Harry
and the Dragon War

Horrible Harry and the Dragon War

BY SUZY KLINE

Pictures by Frank Remkiewicz

PUFFIN BOOKS

PUFFIN BOOKS
Published by Penguin Group
Penguin Young Readers Group,
345 Hudson Street, New York, New York 10014, U.S.A.
Penguin Books Ltd, 80 Strand, London WC2R ORL, England
Penguin Books Australia Ltd, 250 Camberwell Road, Camberwell, Victoria 3124, Australi
Penguin Books Canada Ltd, 10 Alcorn Avenue, Toronto, Ontario, Canada M4V 3B2
Penguin Books (N.Z.) Ltd, 182-190 Wairau Road, Auckland 10, New Zealand

First published in the United States of America by Viking,
a division of Penguin Putnam Books for Young Readers, 2002
Published by Puffin Books,
a division of Penguin Young Readers Group, 2003

23 25 27 26 24 22

Text copyright © Suzy Kline, 2002
Illustrations copyright © Frank Remkiewicz, 2003
All rights reserved

THE LIBRARY OF CONGRESS HAS CATALOGED THE VIKING EDITION AS FOLLOWS:
Kline, Suzy
Horrible Harry and the dragon war / by Suzy Kline ; [Frank Remkiewicz, illustrator].
p. cm.
Summary: Working on a dragon project in Room 3B leads to
a war between two good friends—Harry and Song Lee.
ISBN: 0-670-03559-9 (hc)
[1. Friendship—Fiction. 2. Fighting (Psychology)—Fiction. 3. Schools—Fiction.
4. Korean Americans—Fiction.] I. Remkiewicz, Frank, ill. II. Title.
PZ7.K6797 Hnk 2002 [Fic]—dc21 2001056849

Puffin Books ISBN 0-14-250166-2

Printed in the United States of America

Special thanks to the following people for their valuable help with this manuscript: my editor, Cathy Hennessy; my daughter, Emily Hurtuk; my husband, Rufus; my friend Mary Ann Boulanger; Rhoda Blumberg for her helpful essay, "The Truth about Dragons"; and Rick McBride, Cultural Consultant at the Consulate General of the Republic of Korea in Los Angeles, California.

And special appreciation for the wonderful read-alouds I shared each year with my students: *My Father's Dragon*, *Charlotte's Web*, and *Stone Fox*.

Dedicated to my third grandchild,
Gabrielle Lauren DeAngelis,
born December 1, 2001,
Manchester, New Hampshire

Gabby,
I love you,
Grandma Sue

Contents

Contents

Clouds of War

My name is Doug. I'm in Room 3B. Usually, I write stories about my best friend, Harry. He loves to do horrible things. Sometimes I write about Song Lee. She's the nicest person in third grade. Once I even wrote about Harry and Song Lee getting married.

But that's an old story.

This is a new one and the most horrible one of all. Harry and Song Lee's first fight. A fight that turned into a *war*.

It all started with dragons.

We were sitting on the rug having our morning snack. Harry was eating celery sticks with peanut butter. He says the raisins down the middle are ants on a log. Sidney was munching on his usual, an apple with brown spots.

I was slurping grape juice with my new twisty straw. Miss Mackle, our teacher, was peeling a tangerine when she broke the news. "Our next project is going to be fun. Pick an animal from any story you've read and find out all you can about it."

Mary waved her yogurt spoon in the air. "I know who I'm doing. Charlotte from *Charlotte's Web*! She saved Wilbur's life."

"I'm doing Searchlight from *Stone Fox*," I said. "I love that dog. She helped little Willy and his grandfather save their farm."

"Dibs on Templeton from

Charlotte's Web," Sidney called out. He loves to eat like me!" When Sid bit into another brown spot, Mary cringed.

"Only *you* would choose a rat," she groaned. "But I can see why." Then she pointed to Sid's snack. "You both like rotten things."

Sidney cackled as he wiped the apple juice off his mouth with his shirt sleeve.

Miss Mackle clapped her hands. "I'm so happy some of you already know which animal you want. Anyone else have an idea?"

Song Lee raised her hand. "I *love* dragons. Remember when you read *My Father's Dragon* to us?"

Miss Mackle smiled. "I sure do. It's one of my favorites!"

"I read it again, myself. Could I do my project on dragons?" Song Lee begged.

Before Miss Mackle could say yes, Harry jumped up. His celery went fly-

ing into the air, hit the blackboard, and fell sticky side down on the braided rug.

Song Lee giggled as she helped wipe up the peanut butter mess with her pink napkin.

"My grandmother read *St. George and the Dragon* to me last night. It was cool. See?" Harry whipped the library book out of his backpack. "I want to do dragons, too!"

Everyone looked at the terrifying beast on the cover. It was spitting fire.

"Hmmm . . ." the teacher replied. "Why not? They're mythical animals. You can both do dragons. You and Song Lee work so well together."

While Harry slapped Song Lee five, we all smiled. No one dreamed Miss

Mackle's decision was going to be deadly.

I think the weather knew, though.

Dark clouds circled Southeast School and thunder rolled. When a tree branch tapped our classroom window, we stopped talking and looked up. Was the whistling wind trying to tell us something?

Yes!

Doom was coming to Room 3B!

The "S" Word

That stormy morning Miss Mackle set out toilet paper rolls, balloons, newspaper, cardboard, and masking tape on the supply table. She was at the sink mixing something in a bucket. "I'm excited about this new quick-drying art paste for our papier-mâché. But you need to sketch your animals first."

"Yippee!" Harry and I shouted. We loved doing messy projects. Everyone got busy drawing.

Harry drew a dragon with a huge sail of skin on its back, huge bat wings, five sharp claws, and a spiked tail with a fat arrow at the end. It looked like the picture in his book. It spit fire and poisonous green smoke. "This baby is one mean dragon!" Harry roared.

"Mine's not mean," Song Lee said softly. "He's kind, like the one Elmer talked about in *My Father's Dragon*. Did you know I was born in the Year of the Dragon? It only comes once every twelve years. I was lucky. Dragons bring good fortune!"

Harry put his green crayon down and stared at what Song Lee had drawn. "A blue, green, and yellow striped dragon with curly hair? Four claws and one little red horn? No wings? How can he fly?"

"He flies," Song Lee said proudly. "My dragon has a mane like a lion. It pumps air in and out and helps him fly."

"What's that white round thing in his mouth?" Harry asked.

"That's his pearl. In Korean, we call it *yom ju*. It helps dragons fly, too, but no one knows how."

Harry rolled his eyes. "What's he eating?"

Song Lee smiled. "He's eating bamboo and sipping cream."

"Cream?" Harry laughed. "Don't you know dragons drink elephant's blood? Hercules killed one with a bunch of heads and poisonous breath. Dragons are terrifying! They eat people!"

"Not mine," Song Lee insisted. "My dragon isn't mean. He's gentle. And he loves cream."

Harry shook his head as he watched Song Lee draw flowers on the dragon's bowl.

Then he said it.

One little "s" word that hit our room like a torpedo.

"Your dragon is *stupid!*"

Song Lee immediately glared at Harry. Her eyes got all watery. "My dragon is not stupid. He's beautiful!"

"Beautiful? Dragons are *fierce*. If I lived in the Middle Ages, I'd be Sir Harry! I'd slay the dragon with my silver sword and save you."

Song Lee stood up and made a face that I had never seen before. She was angry and sad at the same time. "I don't need to be saved. I *love* dragons! They bring good luck!" When she blinked, a tear dropped onto her paper and blurred her dragon picture. She quickly pulled out her pink blossom handkerchief, wiped her eyes, and stopped crying. Then she picked up her things and marched over to Ida and Mary's table.

Harry shrugged as he looked at

me. "Hey, Doug, I can't help it if she doesn't know anything about dragons."

I shrugged back. I didn't feel like taking sides. Harry was my best friend, but Song Lee was my friend, too.

When Harry reached for a green crayon, he noticed it looked brand-new. "This has to be hers," he grumbled. "Mine are all stubs." So he brought it over to Song Lee.

"You left this," he mumbled. "You'll need it to color those green stripes on your dragon."

Song Lee didn't look up. She didn't say a word. Mary and I shook our heads. We knew we were watching something awful.

The beginning of a dragon war.

Indoor Rainbow

The next hour was deadly. Nobody laughed. Hardly anybody talked. When we blew up the balloons for our papier-mâché projects, nobody popped one on purpose. Not even Harry.

Miss Mackle noticed Song Lee had moved to the girls' table, but she didn't notice the war. "Everyone's working so nicely together!" she hummed.

"What a wonderful class I have!"

Mary and I exchanged a look. Working nicely together? Song Lee and Harry were working on separate planets.

At 11:05, the rain finally stopped. When the sun peeked out between the clouds, Ida broke the eerie silence. *"Look!"* she screamed. *"There's a rainbow on our table!"*

Everyone shot out of their seat, holding their sticky hands in the air.

There it was.

A perfect little rainbow with all the

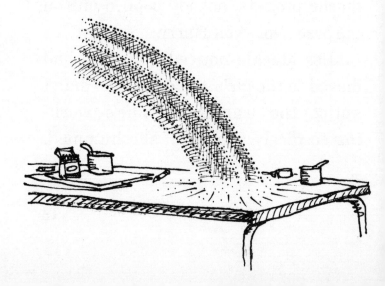

colors: red, orange, yellow, green, blue, indigo, and violet. It was magical!

"See," Song Lee said. "Dragons bring good luck." She was careful to say that to the girls only.

"*Yours* sure does!" Mary replied, clapping her hands. "The rainbow is arched over *your dragon*!"

Harry groaned, "Rainbows, schmainbows. They have nothing to do with luck."

Mary and Ida shot Harry a look.

Sid followed him back to his table. "If you were a leprechaun, Harry, you wouldn't say that. They hide gold at the end of rainbows."

Harry plopped down in his chair. "In case you haven't noticed, Sid the Squid, I'm not a leprechaun. I'm a knight! Sir Harry! See the dragon I'm making?"

"Cool," Sid replied. "So I'll call you Sir Harry the Canary from now on."

Harry nodded as he taped a toilet paper roll onto his dragon. I don't think Harry minded his nickname as much when Sid put "Sir" in front of it.

A few minutes later, Harry walked over to Song Lee. He had forgotten she was mad at him. "What do you think of my dragon now?" he asked.

Song Lee always said something nice about Harry's work.

But this time, it was different.

Song Lee didn't look at Harry. She didn't say *one* word. She just kept pasting long paper strips on her dragon.

Their fight had turned into a deadly silent war. "How long are you going to keep this up?" Harry demanded.

Song Lee said nothing.

The silence was so strong we could hear the wall clock tick tick ticking.

This time when Harry returned to our table, Mary followed him. As soon as he sat down, she shook a finger in his face. "You need to apologize."

"To who?" Harry asked.

"Song Lee!"

"For what?" Harry snapped.

"For calling her dragon *stupid*."

"No way," Harry insisted. "Any dragon that drinks cream and has stripes and curly hair *is* stupid."

Mary blew up into her bangs. She was furious. "Harry Spooger, I am joining Song Lee's side in this war.

Just *you* wait for recess."

Harry grumbled something as Mary stormed off.

Oh boy, I thought. Recess is going to be deadly. I tried to change the subject. "Hey, Harry," I said. "You know what this green goopy stuff looks like?"

Harry didn't respond.

I told him anyway.

"Snot."

I let the gooey paste drip slowly from my long paper strip so he could see what I meant.

"Yeah," Harry replied. He looked over for a second. He didn't laugh like he usually did at gross things. Or fall off his chair. He didn't even flash his white teeth.

Ever since Harry and Song Lee had their big fight, life in Room 3B just wasn't fun anymore.

Outdoor Battle

At noon recess, Mary shouted, "To the kickball diamond!" Everybody ran to the far field. There was only one puddle on the playground, and it was way over by the fence.

As we gathered together, Mary announced, "Today's kickball game is a big one. It's a battle between the dragons! You can either be on Song Lee's side, or on Harry's side."

Harry immediately sprang into action. "Anyone on my team is a Fire-Breathing Dragon with Green Poisonous Breath. Our fierce dragons are going to win!" he bragged.

I knew I'd be on Harry's side. Sidney did, too. He gargled like he was swishing mouthwash. Sid didn't look like a very mean dragon, but he tried.

As people chose sides, Song Lee whispered something into Mary's ear. Mary nodded, then said, "Our team is the G.L.D.'s. The Good-Luck Dragons! And we're up first. Play ball!"

Song Lee waited behind the plate, because in Room 3B, captains kick first. Usually Harry runs out to play centerfield. He likes catching fly balls. Today he stomped.

I moseyed over to shortstop.

No one made small talk or cheered on the team.

Dexter tried to lighten things up. He did a rock-and-roll dance at the mound first, and sang "Bee bop de boo" a few times. Song Lee just waited at the plate.

"Play ball!" Mary shouted.

Dexter sang one more "Bee bop de boo," then rolled a fast ball over the plate.

Song Lee leaped forward to meet it. She kicked the ball hard with her red and white sneakers.

Pow!

Up . . . up . . . up . . . it went! Harry chased it. The ball hit the fence, then bounced back into the puddle.

Splash!

Harry was there for the water-works. He got sprayed right in the face! Song Lee had enough time to race around the bases for a home run while Harry waded into the puddle and fished out the floating ball.

The G.L.D.'s scored their first point. Mary made a slash mark on the cement in white chalk. *"We're ahead!"* she bragged.

Three outs later, the G.L.D.'s were ahead seven to nothing. Song Lee pitched a bouncy fast ball over the plate. Harry ran up to meet it. His sneakers squeaked with water.

Suddenly, an ambulance rounded the corner. Harry turned to look and missed the ball!

When Sid laughed, Harry shot him a look.

Mary yelled, "Strike one!"

"There are no strikeouts in kick-ball," Harry groaned.

"It counts as a foul!" Mary replied. "Remember? We added that rule last month."

Harry grumbled something while Song Lee pitched the next ball. This time she put an extra twist on it. I could tell she was angry. That ball whizzed to the plate!

Harry didn't notice. He was too busy pretending he was a fire-breathing dragon. He exhaled loudly and roared as he ran toward the spinning ball.

Bloop!

Harry's kick went up over his head and backward into foul territory.

"Two fouls!" Mary screamed, holding

up two fingers. "One more and you're out."

Harry's eyes looked like red-hot coals.

Song Lee pitched another wicked spinner.

Harry flapped his arms like they were huge bat wings and went charging after the ball.

Wham!

The ball went up, up, up, then down, down, down by the left side of the fence.

"Three fouls! You're out!" Mary yelled.

Harry stomped to the end of the line and faced the oak tree on the other side of the fence. All you could see was his back. That's what Harry does when he thinks he might cry. He doesn't want anyone to know.

When the bell rang, we were behind six to seven. The Fire-Breathing Dragons with Green Poisonous Breath had run out of time. Harry kicked the fence three times. Boy, was he mad!

Sidney was, too. He walked up to Harry and pointed to his chest. "If it weren't for *you*, and your *stupid* kicking, we could have won!"

That did it! Harry jumped on Sid's back and rode him around like a wild bronco. His wet shoes made marks on Sid's pants.

"Get off! Get off me!" Sidney shouted.

Mary rushed over to Harry. "So . . ." she scolded. "How do *you* like it when someone calls *you* stupid?"

Harry didn't answer.

He just slid off Sid's back and looked over at Song Lee. She had her head down. Winning the game didn't change anything. Song Lee's mood was either mad or sad. She didn't feel like slapping her team five.

"Gee," Ida complained, "even kickball isn't fun anymore."

"I know," Mary groaned. "Nothing is."

"Yeah," I agreed. "I hate war."

Harry didn't say a word to anyone. He just walked to the cafeteria alone.

The White Package

Everyone knows when you surrender, you hold up a white flag. That's what happens in real wars. And that's what finally happened in Room 3B.

Sort of.

The white part anyway.

It just wasn't a flag.

Room 3B was sitting in the cafeteria. It was hot-dog day and most of us were eating hot dogs. Sidney sat at the end of the table, far away from Harry. I think both of them regretted using the "s" word.

"Rats! I didn't get any mustard," Harry said. "Come with me, Doug."

I jumped out of my seat. I was happy Harry was talking again.

I got a little worried, though, as I followed him. We didn't join the student line. We walked farther down, to the teachers' side of the cafeteria.

"Hey, Harry," I asked. "What are you doing?"

"Getting something white," he whispered.

White? I took one quick look at the glass shelf. There was yogurt and cream cheese that was white, but Harry didn't take anything from that shelf. He took

something that was next to the coffee
urn. As soon as he stuffed it into his
pants pocket, we took off!

When we returned to our table,
Harry reached in his pants pocket,

pulled out a packet of mustard, and squeezed some on his hot dog.

Harry had it all along!

At 12:45, our class went back to the room. Miss Mackle always gives us fifteen minutes of activity time after lunch. Mary was helping Song Lee look up stuff about dragons on the computer. Each time they found something, they printed out a page.

Harry went over to the supply table and wrapped the surprise he had in his pocket. He used white paper and plenty of Scotch tape. The package looked like a wrinkled baseball. He wrote something on a piece of paper, folded it in half, and taped it on top of the package.

I watched Harry creep over to Song Lee's table and set that white package right next to her striped dragon. He was giving Song Lee a gift!

At that very moment, shrieks came from the front of the room. "Wow!" Mary exclaimed. "Listen to this you guys!" she called out.

Dexter and I left our checker game and joined the crowd gathering around the computer.

"The Western dragons are terrifying!" Mary read. "Many of them are in stories from Africa and Europe."

Harry clasped his fists together and waved them over his head like he was a champion. "I knew it!" he said. "I knew it all along!"

Mary continued. "Their bodies are filled with venom! Their favorite drink is milk, and . . ." Mary shuddered, "aaaaauuugh . . . they eat maidens, birds, oxen, and deer, and enjoy cakes and elephant's blood."

"*Yeah!*" Harry roared, racing back to our table to get his dragon.

Miss Mackle was smiling as she joined us at the computer. She loved it when her students discovered facts on their own.

"Wait a minute," Mary said, holding up a finger. "There is another kind of dragon . . . the Eastern dragon— and they are beautiful, friendly, and wise!"

Song Lee made prayer hands while Harry took a step back, hugged his

dragon, and frowned. Mary kept reading. "Some Asian cities have New Year's parades with dragons leading them. These dragons are loved and worshipped! They breathe clouds, eat bamboo and cream, and get fat on arsenic. Arsenic will poison humans, but not dragons."

"Oooooooh," we said.

"Cool!" I said.

At one o'clock, activity time was over and we had to go back to our seats and gather facts about our other animals.

Mary hogged the computer to do spider research. I grabbed the D encyclopedia. Sid grabbed volume R.

As soon as she returned to her table, Song Lee spotted the white package. She untaped the note and

started reading it. Harry whispered
the words to me:

Dear Song Lee,
I'm sorry I called
your dragon stoopid.

Here is something
for him to drink.
            Harry

We watched Song Lee unwrap the
white, wrinkly paper. A small plastic
creamer rolled out onto her desk. It

was the kind teachers use for their coffee. When Song Lee pretended to pour it into her dragon's mouth, Harry flashed a toothy smile.

Yes! The old Harry was back!

Song Lee rushed over to Mary and showed her Harry's note. Mary hugged her. "I don't believe it!" she said. "Harry apologized. And made a peace offering, too. We should celebrate the end of our war."

"I know just what to do," Song Lee said.

The Dragon Parade

A minute later, Song Lee came over to Harry. He greeted her with a smile as U-shaped as a slice of cantaloupe.

Song Lee made her dragon hop three times on the table. Then she turned his head to face Harry's dragon.

"Thank you for my cream. But where's my bamboo?" she giggled.

Harry made his dragon reply in a

deep, ferocious voice. "I'll get you a Pop-sicle stick tomorrow."

The silent war was over! Song Lee and Harry were talking to each other. At least their dragons were. It was better than any fireworks on the Fourth of July!

"I know how we can celebrate," Mary said. "We could have a parade. The two kinds of dragons can lead it, just like a New Year's parade."

"What a great idea!" Miss Mackle

called out. She was standing at the sink, scrubbing the bucket of paste. "We can celebrate our works in progress. Why don't we snake our line right down the hall to the library. Mrs. Michaelsen, our librarian, would love it."

"Ruff! Ruff!" I said making Searchlight bark. I loved how I was painting her. Just like the story! All black with one white spot on her forehead the size of a silver dollar.

"Grrrrr . . . grrrr!" Ida growled for her yellow mongoose from *Rikki Tikki Tavi*. I loved the snake she put in its mouth.

Song Lee and Harry went to the front of the line. Dexter hung out with me.

"Hey, Dex," I asked, "how come you picked the goose in *Charlotte's Web*?"

"Why do you think?" he answered. "Because of Elvis. You know how I read everything about him. I love rock and roll."

"Everybody knows that," I replied. "But why geese?"

"Elvis had them in his yard. He knew goose poop helped his garden grow."

"Cool," I said.

"Let's get this show on the road," Sidney complained. "I can't wait for

Mrs. Michaelsen to see my Templeton. I even put Charlotte's egg sack in his mouth. *'Thith thtuff thticks in my mouth. It'th worth than caramel candy.'"*

"That's pretty good, Sid," I said.

That afternoon we were so happy, holding our animals high, marching down the hall. When we got halfway, Harry said his dragon was thirsty, so he borrowed Song Lee's creamer. After he peeled back the white top, he gave his dragon a sip, then passed it back to Song Lee. "Both of our dragons love this stuff," Harry said.

Song Lee smiled.

By the time we got to the library, the dragons had milk mustaches.

Harry and Song Lee did, too.

I don't think the teacher ever knew

what the real celebration was about.
She and Mrs. Michaelsen were oooh-
ing and ahhhing about the papier-
mâché animals.

But we knew.

Harry and Song Lee's friendship sur-
vived the Dragon War. And so did the
rest of us in Room 3B!